Prentice-Hall International,Inc., London
Prentice-Hall of Australia, Pty. Ltd., Sydney
Prentice-Hall Canada, Inc., Toronto
Prentice-Hall of India Private Ltd., New Delhi
Prentice-Hall of Japan, Inc., Tokyo
Prentice-Hall of Southeast Asia Pte. Ltd., Singapore
Whitehall Books Limited, Wellington, New Zealand
Editora Prentice-Hall do Brasil LTDA., Rio de Janeiro
Prentice-Hall Hispanoamericana, S.A., Mexico

10 9 8 7 6 5 4 3 2 1

Library of Congress Cataloging in Publication Data
Asch, Frank.      Bear shadow.
Summary: Bear tries everything he can think of
to get rid of his shadow.
1. Children's stories, American.  [1. Bears—
Fiction.  2. Shadows—Fiction]  I. Title.
PZ7.A778Be  1984   [E]   84-18250
ISBN 0-13-071580-8

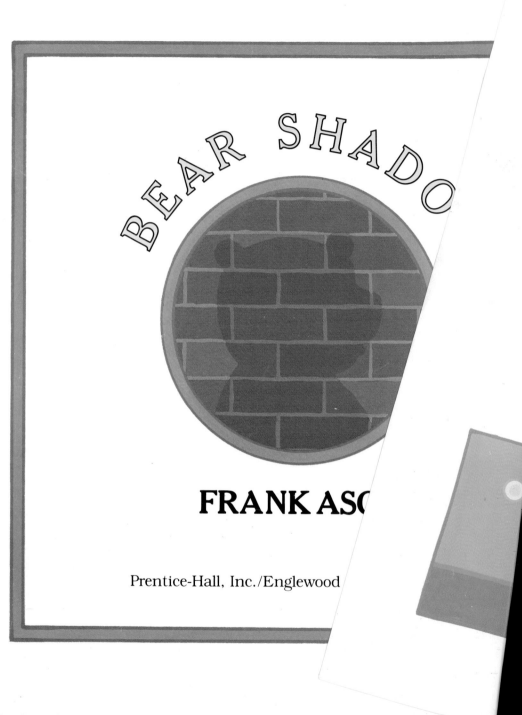

# BEAR SHADO

## FRANK AS

Prentice-Hall, Inc./Englewood

To Devin

One day Bear went down to the pond with his
fishing pole and a big can of worms. While he
was putting a worm on his hook, he looked
down and saw a big fish. I'm going to
catch that fish, thought Bear to himself.

But when Bear stood up to throw his line in
the water, his shadow scared the big fish away.
"Go away, Shadow!" cried Bear.
But Bear's shadow would not go away.

"Okay," said Bear. "If you won't go on your own, then I'll just have to get rid of you!" And he put down his fishing pole and began to run. He ran around the pond. When he got to the other side he kept on running.

He ran through a field of flowers, jumped over the brook and hid behind a tree.

"Good!" thought Bear. "Now Shadow can't find me!"

But Bear was wrong.
When he stepped out from behind the tree
the first thing he saw was Shadow.

Nearby was a cliff. Bear walked over to the
cliff and looked up. I'll climb so high
Shadow won't be able to follow me, thought Bear.

Bear climbed higher and higher until
at last he pulled himself up to the top.
Huffing and puffing, he smiled with pride.
Then he looked down and saw Shadow.

Now Bear was very annoyed, so he went home
and got a hammer and some nails
to nail his shadow to the ground.

He hammered and hammered and hammered,
but no matter how many nails he hammered,
he couldn't nail his shadow down.

If I can't nail him down, thought Bear,
maybe I can bury him. So he got his shovel
and dug a hole. When the hole was deep and wide,
he let his shadow fall in the hole.

Then Bear filled in the hole with dirt.
When he was finished it was almost noon.
The sun was high in the sky and
Shadow was nowhere to be seen.
"At last!" sighed Bear. "No more shadow!"

But now Bear was very tired.

So he went inside and took a little nap.

While he slept, time passed and the sun

once again cast shadows everywhere.

When Bear got up and opened his door,
he saw his shadow on the floor.
"Not you again!" exclaimed Bear.
And he slammed the door, hoping to lock
Shadow inside. But Shadow was too quick.

"Mmm," sighed Bear, "How about this...
If you let me catch a fish,
I'll let you catch one, too.
Nod your head like this if it's a deal."
When Bear nodded his head, Shadow nodded too.

So Bear went back to the pond and
once again threw his line in the water.
By this time the sun was in a different
part of the sky, which made it easy for
Shadow to keep his part of the deal.

And when Bear caught that big fish,
Shadow caught one too.

E        Asch, Frank
ASC      Bear shadow